Young Readers

LEVEL 1

EWOKS JOIN THE FIGHT

WRITTEN BY MICHAEL SIGLAIN

EGMONT

We bring stories to life

First published in Great Britain 2016
by Egmont UK Limited, The Yellow Building,
1 Nicholas Road, London W11 4AN.

© & TM 2016 Lucasfilm Ltd.

ISBN 978 1 4052 7784 6
60534/1
Printed in Singapore

To find more great *Star Wars* books, visit www.egmont.co.uk/starwars

Stay safe online. Any website addresses listed in this book are correct at the
time of going to print. However, Egmont is not responsible for content hosted by
third parties. Please be aware that online content can be subject to change and
websites can contain content that is unsuitable for children. We advise that all
children are supervised when using the internet.

High above the forest moon
was the Empire's secret weapon.
The secret weapon was
a new Death Star.

The rebels sent Han, Luke, Leia
and Chewie on a mission to the
forest moon.

The rebels had to find a bunker.
Inside the bunker was a machine.
The machine kept the Death Star
safe. The rebels had to destroy
the machine.

The rebels searched for the bunker.
The rebels saw two biker scouts.
The biker scouts patrolled the forest.
They also guarded the bunker.

Han and Chewie had to stop
the biker scouts.
They did not want the
biker scouts to warn the Empire.

The biker scouts escaped.
Luke and Leia jumped on
speeder bikes.

They chased the biker scouts.

Luke and Leia split up.

Luke used his lightsaber.

Luke stopped one biker scout.

Then he returned to the rebels.

Leia stopped the other
biker scout.
But their fight broke her speeder.
Leia was lost in the forest.

A small creature approached Leia.

It was an Ewok.

Ewoks are small and furry.

They live in the forest.

Leia gave the Ewok some food.
Then a hidden biker scout
attacked. The Ewok helped Leia
stop the scout.

Leia and the Ewok were now friends. The Ewok took Leia to his village.

Han, Luke and Chewie searched
the forest for Leia.
They took R2-D2 and C-3PO
with them.

In the forest was a trap.

The rebels walked into the trap.

The rebels were stuck in a net.

R2-D2 cut them down.

The rebels landed on the ground.
They saw the Ewoks.
The Ewoks had set the trap.

The Ewoks tied up the rebels.
The Ewoks took the rebels
to their village.

Then Leia appeared.

She told the Ewoks that the rebels were her friends.

The Ewoks did not listen to her.

Luke knew what to do.
He knew that the Ewoks could
help them. Luke used the Force.

Luke made C-3PO float
through the air.

The Ewoks were scared.
They thought C-3PO
had special powers.
The Ewoks freed the rebels.

The rebels learned that Chief Chirpa was the leader of the Ewoks. And the Ewok who had helped Leia was named Wicket.

C-3PO told the Ewoks
all about the rebels.
The Ewoks liked the rebels.
They did not like the
biker scouts.

The Ewoks agreed to help
the rebels.
The rebels were now
a part of the tribe.

The Ewoks took the rebels
to the hidden bunker.
The rebels surprised the
biker scouts.

But inside the bunker were
more biker scouts.
They were waiting for
the rebels.

The rebels had been captured.
It was time for the Ewoks
to join the fight!

There was a big battle.

The Ewoks helped the rebels.

The Ewoks and the rebels fought hard. They stopped the biker scouts. They destroyed the bunker.

The rebels destroyed the
new Death Star.
The rebels and the Ewoks
saved the day!